PEDDLES

For my pal Jean Z.,
who, like Peddles, knows how to give back

SIMON & SCHUSTER BOOKS FOR YOUNG READERS
An imprint of Simon & Schuster Children's Publishing Division
1230 Avenue of the Americas, New York, New York 10020
Copyright © 2016 by Elizabeth Rose Stanton
SIMON & SCHUSTER BOOKS FOR YOUNG READERS is a trademark of Simon & Schuster, Inc.
For information about special discounts for bulk purchases, please contact Simon & Schuster
Special Sales at 1-866-506-1949 or business@simonandschuster.com.
The Simon & Schuster Speakers Bureau can bring authors to your live event.
For more information or to book an event, contact the Simon & Schuster
Speakers Bureau at 1-866-248-3049 or visit our website at www.simonspeakers.com.
Book design by Lucy Ruth Cummins
The text for this book is set in Myster.
The illustrations for this book are rendered in pencil and watercolor.
Manufactured in China
1015 SCP
2 4 6 8 10 9 7 5 3 1
Library of Congress Cataloging-in-Publication Data
Stanton, Elizabeth Rose, author, illustrator.
Peddles / Elizabeth Rose Stanton. — First edition.
pages cm
"A Paula Wiseman book."
Summary: "Peddles is a pig with big ideas—he wants to be a dancer"— Provided by publisher.
ISBN 978-1-4814-1691-7 (hardcover) — ISBN 978-1-4814-1692-4 (ebook)
[1. Pigs—Fiction. 2. Dance—Fiction.] I. Title.
PZ7.S79326Pe 2015
[E]—dc23
2014025142

PEDDLES

Elizabeth Rose Stanton

A PAULA WISEMAN BOOK · SIMON & SCHUSTER BOOKS FOR YOUNG READERS

New York London Toronto Sydney New Delhi

Peddles was just a pig.

He lived on a farm with the other pigs,
doing the usual pig things:

eating and sleeping

and oinking and rooting

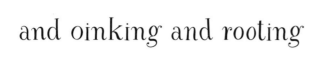

and wallowing

and . . .

But Peddles thought about

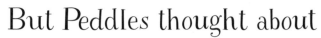

the usual pig things

differently.

Peddles had ideas—

big ideas.

The other pigs would shake their heads at him and say,

"Get your head out of the clouds, Peddles," and "Stop being so spacey."

This gave Peddles even BIGGER ideas.

But nothing ever happened . . .

until one night . . .

Peddles heard whooping and hollering.

He saw twirling and whirling.

He saw boots stomping and feet kicking up high.

Peddles had an IDEA!

He thought it might be possible.

After all,

if a cat could fiddle

and a cow could jump over the moon,

why couldn't *he* . . .

DANCE?

BUT something was missing.

So he tromped and
plodded. He thudded
and clunked. He
bumbled and lumbered
and clattered . . .

and borrowed.

But he didn't dance.

He kept on rooting around, looking *for* ideas,

when he *found* a bag behind the barn.

Peddles thought it might be a good idea to root through it.

At the very bottom, he found

them.

Off he clomped, back to the barnyard.

It didn't go well.

Just when Peddles was beginning to think it had been a bad idea,

he felt a nudge—

then another, and another.

Back and *forth* and back and *forth*, they nudged and pushed and pushed and nudged until Peddles was back up on his *feet!*

Together, they trotted back to the pigpen with a little detour, first, to behind the barn.

And that turned out to be

the best idea of all!